GERY WOLF

DAS STEIRISCHE

WeinLAND

Seite 6/7: Die „steirische Toskana“ aus der Luft
Aerial view of the ”Styrian Tuscany“

Seite 8/9: Rebstöcke im Winterkleid
Vines in their wintercoat

Seite 10/11: Abendstimmung in der
Gegend von Berghausen
Romantic evening hour near Berghausen

Seite 12/13: Die Packer Kapelle zwischen Gamlitz
und Leutschach
The chapel of Pack between Gamlitz
and Leutschach

Seite 14/15: Frühlingsbeginn im Weinland
The first days of spring in the wine-growing
region

WOLFGANG SOTILL

Der lange Weg zur Leichtigkeit

Orte brauchen Zeiten. Kirchen den feierlichen Sonntag, Venedig den nebeligen November, die Südsteiermark den überreich sonnigen August. Da liegen jene Gäste, die später im Jahr der Maroni und des aufwallenden „Sturms" wegen in das Land an der Grenze kommen, noch weiter im Süden. Sie räkeln sich am Meer, dem ebenfalls der Sommer zugeordnet wird. Im August stehen die schwarzen Sportcabrios noch nicht in den Rebgassen und die zartbetufteten Damen, die stets nach Gastroführern und nicht nach eigenem Geschmack die besten Weine zu benennen wissen, flüstern den Winzern noch keine weinseligen Versprechungen zu: „Ach, wenn Sie einmal in Wien sind, dann ..."
Übrigens: Weil guter, auf Muschelerde gewachsener Sauvignon blanc gar rasch Gefühle zu erheben im Stande ist, soll die plötzliche erotische Zuneigung ungeprüft, und somit irrtümlich,auch schon manchem Schankbursch zugefallen sein. Der daraufhin höchst verwundert bemerkt hat: „Mei, waun kumb unserans ba der vüln Arbeit scho auf Wien?" Die Gegend kennt also auch den bitteren Witz. Es ist also der August, in dem man das Land besucht – er ist der rechte Zeitpunkt. Der Wein vom Vorjahr ist in der Flasche schon ruhig geworden, die nobeligen Gäste fehlen noch und die Weinbauern haben jetzt leichter Zeit als im Herbst. Vor der letzten Reife des Septembers haben sie nur eines zu tun: zu warten. Dies ist kein entspanntes sich der Muße hingeben, sondern ein zur Untätigkeit gezwungen sein. Die Winzer können, selbst wenn sie es wünschten, nichts beschleunigen und auch nichts intensivieren, sondern nur auf letzte kräftigende Sonnentage hoffen. Nicht selten mischt sich in diese Hoffnung tiefes Bangen. Kein Wunder, dass Bauern oft religiöser sind als Städter.
Der August mit seiner gleißenden Sonne, die duftend Thymian verströmt und auch Heu, das wir später in trockenen Traminern wiederfinden, verwehrt uns die romantische Sicht auf das Land zwischen Spielfeld und Leutschach. Auf jene verschlungenen und sich verwindenden Hügel, die

von bemühten Literaten als „steirische Toskana“ oder gar als „zweite Wachau“ bezeichnet werden. Den Touristikern, nicht aber den Bewohnern der Region, war der Vergleich mit der Pappel bestandenen Landschaft Italiens, wie auch jener mit dem niederösterreichischen Flusstal nur recht. Hauptsache, die Gegend, in der Weingärten so steil sind, dass neben dem obersten Rebstock die Paragleiter abheben, erhielt ein süsslich-liebliches Image. Und Hauptsache auch, das Grenzland zu Slowenien verlor den bitteren Beigeschmack vom An-den-Rand-gedrängt-Sein.

„Papa, hast den Reisepass eingepackt?“ lautete lange Zeit die besorget Frage jener Steirer, die nördlich von Leibnitz beheimatet, bloß einmal im Jahr in die Südsteiermark kamen. In jene Region, die sie ein wenig verächtlich – oder war es doch nur politische Unkenntnis – auch als Untersteiermark bezeichneten. Man reiste an, um billig Wein zu kaufen und Brettljausn zu bestellen, die so groß waren, dass der Papa am Montag noch etwas davon „in die Schicht“ mitnehmen konnte. Und deswegen war es notwendig, neben dem Reisepass auch gleich die Alufolie miteinzupacken. Die bewirtende Bäuerin freute sich über „so ane nettn Gäst, denen's bei uns g'fallt und schmeckt“. Und weil sie gar sicher sein wollte, dass die Obersteirer auch im nächsten Jahr wiederkommen, schmuggelte sie zwischen die verkauften Weinflaschen noch rasch ein paar Selchwürstel hinein – eine fette Erinnerung.

Lange war das Leben an der Grenze ein wenig armselig und die Menschen untertänig, ohne Selbstbewusstsein und für alles dankbar. Herrenbauern gab es immer nur in der Obersteiermark.

Weil der „Papa“, mutig geworden nach ein paar Glaserl, seinen Reisepass nicht umsonst mitgenommen haben wollte, hielt er in Ratsch an der Weinstraße an, zückte Pass und Kodak Instamatic und stellte sich vor die Tafel, auf der zweisprachig zu lesen steht: „Achtung Staatsgrenze. Über 400 Meter verläuft die Grenze inmitten der Straße“. Da stand er nun, breitbeinig, die eine Hälfte in Slowenien, die andere in Österreich. Bald würde er das Bild seinen Arbeitskollegen zeigen, um zu beweisen, wie mutig er war. Dabei wird er verschweigen, dass er immer am Sprung auf die heimatliche Seite war. Die Südsteiermark als das halb-halb Erlebnis des kleinen Mannes, der sich dasselbe am Äquator nicht zu leisten vermag.

Seit sich im Juni 1991 Slowenien vom jugoslawischen Zentralstaat losgesagt hat, braucht der zwei-Staaten-zugleich-Besucher nicht mehr zu fürchten, dass plötzlich eine Patrouille aus dem Busch springt, „stoj“ und auch noch so etwas wie „Kontrolla“ ruft.

Im Jahr 1991 hat der imaginäre Strich, der seit den Friedensverträgen von 1919 deutlich zwischen hüben und drüben, zwischen uns und denen unterschied, unter den Einheimischen seinen Schrecken verloren. Gezogen war er seinerzeit bei der Konferenz von St. Germain entlang der Pfarrgrenzen worden, die zugleich auch die Sprachgrenzen waren. So weiß es die Geschichtsschreibung, in der leider nie die wirklich entscheidenden Dinge des Lebens ihre Berücksichtigung finden: eine halbe Sau, ein paar Flaschen Schnaps. Denn mittels solcher Bestechung gelang es so manchem Bauern, dessen Hof „nach unten" hätte fallen sollen, sich doch „nach oben" zu retten. Noch heute führt die Zufahrt zu diesen Höfen über slowenisches Territorium. Was den Nachteil hatte, dass während des slowenischen Unabhängigkeitskampfes das österreichische Bundesheer zur Verteidigung solcher Höfe zu Fuß anmarschieren musste. Vorsichtshalber ließ man gleich auch die Waffen zurück. Mit bewaffneten Soldaten über slowenische Straßen zu fahren, wäre eine Neutralitätsverletzung gewesen.

Die Pinnitsch und die Stanis, die Sabbatis und die Gradisniks sind alle froh, herüben zu wohnen – so, wie sie es immer waren. Nur manchmal regen sich die längst verschüttet geglaubten Sehnsüchte wieder. Nämlich, wenn die slowenischen Südsteirer unter sich sind. Bei Taufen, Hochzeiten und Begräbnissen. Dann stimmen sie ihre alten Weisen an, die in sich ganz wunderbar Lebensfreude und Schwermut zugleich vereinen. Und wer, wie die meisten Jungen heute die Lieder nicht mehr kann und die Texte auch nicht versteht, weil es lange nicht schick war, die eigene Sprache an die Kinder weiterzugeben, der geht wenigstens am Pfingstsonntag über die Grenze hinauf nach Sveti Duh. Nach „Heilig Geist", um dort zum Pfarrpatrozinium die slowenische Messe mit ihren getragenen Gesängen mitzufeiern. Der danach abgehaltene deutsche Gottesdienst findet bei weitem nicht so viele Kirchgeher. Dass der Ort in alten Karten nur als „Duh", als „Geist" aufscheint, hat mit dem staatlich verordneten Agnostizismus zu tun, in dem nichts heilig sein durfte, außer dem System selbst. Die Grenznähe hatte auch ihre Vorteile – vor allem, wenn man sie in Zeiten, in denen der Kaffee in Jugoslawien rar war, nutzen konnte, um ein wenig zu schmuggeln. Man legte die Kilopakete in den Kofferraum eines Wagens, am nächsten Tag fand sich dort Geld – hinterlegt von den Grenzsoldaten, die im Schutze der Nacht den Austausch vornahmen. Derartige Gunsterweise ließen die Grenzer, die oft genug aus Serbien stammten, auch nicht ganz so streng sein, wenn zwei Nachbarn, einer von drüben, einer von herüben, zeitgleich mit ihren Traktoren von ihren Höfen aufbrachen, um sich gut getarnt im Wald zu verabreden. Dort hängten sie dann ihre überdachten Anhänger um, von denen der slowenische leer, der steirische aber schwer mit Ziegeln und Zement beladen war. Die Bauutensilien, die dem Slowenen von der sozialistischen Planwirtschaft zwar versprochen, aber nie geliefert worden waren, stellte der Nachbar aus Leutschach. Nun konnte – unabhängig von Marburg, Laibach und Belgrad – der Stallbau doch noch abgeschlossen werden.

Fährt man heute in die Südsteiermark, dann ist sie tatsächlich so, wie der rasche Besucher sie empfindet: leicht, unbeschwert, voll Freude. Vor allem, – sie hat sich bislang noch immer dem Tourismus versagt. Wer hierher kommt und in einer guten Buschenschank, wie bei den Brüdern Hannes und Ewald Zweytick, zukehrt, der ist nicht Kunde, der ist Gast.

Einer, der bewirtet wird, wie es die mittlerweile offen gewordenen Menschen an der offenen Grenzen gerne tun. Sie zeigen her was sie besitzen, sind stolz, keine Geheimnisse zu haben und erzählen enthusiastisch und mit Worten der Ehrfurcht vom Wein. Sie tun es wie Philosophen, die dem Wesen des Seins nachspüren. Auch diese suchen nicht zuerst den Ertrag, sondern den Weg zu ihm. Schmückendes Beiwerk wird weggelassen, um zum Kern vorzudringen. In jenes Zentrum der Erkenntnis, das schon die Römer in das Sprichwort fassten: „Im Wein die Wahrheit".

Die Tements und Polz, die Sattlers und Sabbatis gehören zu den neuen Bauern, die das Erdige wiederentdeckt haben, ohne das Braun-Klumpige an ihren Füssen kleben zu haben. Und so machen sie auch Wein. Sie schaffen es, die Landschaft in die Bouteille zu bringen und dabei so verspielt zu tüfteln, dass die Genießer die Weinstraße in der Erinnerung entlang wandern, wenn sie zu Hause auch Monate später noch eine Flasche Morillon öffnen. Es ist alles in dem Wein, was das Land bietet: Körper, Kraft, Finesse und Charakter. Und vor allem unbändige Lust. Eine Erotik, die vieles in sich aufgesogen hat und die so übervoll ist, dass sie aus sich selbst Träume gebiert. Diesen gilt es sich behutsam zu erschließen. Sie vertragen keine frontale Annäherung, sind sie doch auch flüchtig wie der Duft frischer Maroni, wie das Aroma heranreifenden Quitten. Und sie sind zart, wie die Kleider des Lichts, die sich die Hügel jeden Tag verschwenderisch auf Neue überstülpen. Aber sie sind voll der Berührung und des sich berühren Lassens.

So wie man den Dom in seiner Stille besucht, und sich darauf freut, die Orgel zu hören, und wie man Venedig im November bereist, um in der nebeligen Stadt an die frohen Masken des Faschings zu denken, so besucht man die Südsteiermark – außer im August – auch im Frühjahr. Dann sprießt das junge Gras und die ersten Brennnessel lassen nach langen geruchslosen Wintern Intensität verspüren. Solch frohe Empfindungen lassen vergessen, wie lang der Weg von der harten Grenze bis zur unbeschwerten Leichtigkeit war.

WOLFGANG SOTILL

The long way to lightness

Places need their times. Churches need the festive Sunday, Venice needs its foggy November, the South of Styria needs the lavishly sunny August. Those guests who come to the area near the borders later in the year to enjoy the "Maroni" (roasted chestnuts) and the bubbling "Sturm" (an intermediate product of the alcoholic fermentation process), still lie under the sun further south lazily sunning themselves on the seaside, another thing that belongs to summer. In the summertime, there are no black sports cars in the small streets of the vineyards and no fragrant ladies, who always name the best wines according to the latest wine guides and not to their own tastes. They're not tipsy enough yet to make promises to the wine-grower, "Well, if you happen to come to Vienna, then ...".

By the way, because the Sauvignon blanc growing on old fertile soil is able to rouse quick feelings, these sudden erotic affections are sometimes passed thoughtlessly and thus often mistakenly to the man behind the bar who happens to be just the waiter and not the owner. He would then answer a bit astonished "Mei, woun kumb unserans ba der vüln Arbeit scho auf Wien?" (in Styrian dialect – Well, with this amount of work, there is not much time to go to Vienna often). Apparently, the area also knows bitter irony.

It's August when you come to visit the country – it's just the right time. The wine from last year has calmed down in the bottles, the noble guests haven't arrived yet and the wine-growers have more time off now than in autumn. Before the last ripening in September they have only one thing to do: wait. It is not a relaxing, leisurely way of waiting but a restless one, forced to do nothing. The wine-growers can't expedite anything and can't intensify anything, even if they wished to. They can only hope for some last fortifying sunny days. Very often deep fearfulness mingles with this hope. No wonder farmers are often more religious than people from the towns.

The August with its gleaming sun, the perfume of thyme and also hay, which we can find later in the dry "Traminer", keeps us away from the romantic view over the landscape between Spielfeld and Leutschach, on those entwined and winding hills which some committed writers called the "Styrian Tuscany" or even the "second Wachau". The tourism officials, but not the inhabitants of the region, can only agree with this comparison of Southern Styria with the Italian landscape and the Lower Austrian valley of the Danube. The main thing is that the area where the hills are is so steep that you can see hang-gliders rising from the highest wines composing a sweet and lovely image. The other main thing is that the border area to Slovenia has lost its bitter taste of being put to the edge.

"Daddy, have you got your passport?" For long this was the question of concerned Styrians living north of Leibnitz who only came to the south once a year. In those days it was the region they contemptuously called the "Untersteiermark" – or was it just pure ignorance about the political history. They came to buy cheap wine and to order a "Brettljausn" (an assortment of meat, sausages and bread spread), which was so huge that Daddy was still able to carry the remains to his shift on Monday. Therefore it was necessary to pack not only the passport but also some aluminium foil. The hostess was very happy about "so ane nettn Gäst, denen's bei uns g'fallt und schmeckt" (in Styrian dialect – such nice guests that like us and our food). And because she wanted to make sure that the people from the north of Styria returned the following year, she used to hide some "Selchwürstel" (smoked sausages) in between the bottles of wine the guests had just bought – a greasy souvenir, so to say.

For a long period life close to the border was a bit poor and the people were submissive without self-confidence and thankful for everything. Proud landowners could only be found in the northern part of Styria.

Because Daddy found himself very courageous after some glasses of wine, and he didn't want to carry back his passport without using it, he stop in Ratsch on the wine trail, hold out his document, fish out a Kodak Instamatic and pose in front of the sign which read in two languages "Warning – Border crossing. For 400 metres the border runs in the middle of the road." There he stood, one leg in Slovenia, the other one in Austria. Soon he would show the picture to his colleagues at work to prove how brave he had been. Yet he wouldn't tell them that he had always been prepared to jump onto the side of his native country. Southern Styria as "half-half" adventure for the small man who cannot afford to experience the same thrill at the equator.

Since June 1991, when Slovenia proclaimed itself independent from the Yugoslav central state, the "two-nation-visitor" doesn't have to fear that a patrol suddenly jumps out of

the bushes shouting “stoj” (stop) or even something like “Kontrolla” (control).
The imaginary line set according to the peace treaty from 1919 and clearly distinguishing between “herc” and “there” lost its horror in 1991. At the peace conference in St. Germain way back in 1919 the line was drawn along the borders of the congregations which were at the same time language borders. That’s what history tells us leaving out the really important things of life which were never mentioned: half part of a pork, some bottles of “Schnaps” (liquor). With such means of bribery some farmers were successful in saving their lands to the “upper” side (to the Austrian part) which should have already stayed “down” (and been on the Yugoslavian side). Even today the access to these farms is only reachable through Slovenian territory. This caused a big problem in the course of the Slovenian independence war when the Austrian army had to walk on foot in order to defend these farms. Just to make sure, the soldiers even left behind their weapons. Why? Because crossing the Slovenian border with armed forces would have been an offence against the Austrian neutrality.
The Pinnitsch and the Stanis, the Sabbatis and the Gradisniks are all very happy to live “on this side” – as they used to be. Only sometimes the longings, which were thought to be long forgotten, find their way back, namely when Slovenian Styrians are amongst themselves, at baptisms, weddings and at funerals. Then they start singing their old songs that wonderfully unite the joy of life and the melancholy. And those who don’t know the songs or don’t understand the lyrics – as it is the case for most of the young people because it wasn’t “the fashion” to teach the children the mother tongue – those at least walk up to “Sveti Duh” at Whitsunday crossing the borders between Styria and Slovenia. They go to “Holy Ghost” (Sveti Duh) in order to celebrate the “patron of the church” with a Slovenian mass and stately songs. After that there is usually a mass held in German but its by far not as popular as the Slovenian one. In some of the old maps you can only find “Duh” (“ghost“) which dates from the former state policy of agnosticism in which nothing was allowed to be “holy” except the system itself.
The closeness to the border has also its advantages – especially in times when you could use it to smuggle e.g. coffee which was very rare in Yugoslavia. You would put some kilos of coffee into the boot of the car and park it close to the border. On the next day you would find some money – put there by the border guards who used the dead of night for the exchange.
The same motivation caused guards, coming very often even from Serbia, to look the other way when two neighbours from “this side” and “the other side” left theirs farms with their tractors at the same time in order to meet somewhere in a hidden place in the woods. There they exchanged

their trailers – the Slovenian empty, but the Styrian heavily laden with bricks and cement. The building material was actually promised by the socialist planned economy but never delivered, so the neighbour from Leutschach provided it. Finally it was possible – independent from Maribor, Ljubljana, and Belgrade – to finish the stables.

If you go to Southern Styria today, you can be sure that it really is as it appears to the visitor at a first quick glance – it's easy-going, light-hearted, and full of joy. And above all: the region hasn't been tempted by the big tourist industry yet. Those who arrive there and go to a good Buschenschank, e.g. to the brothers Hannes and Ewald Zweytick, are not customers, they are guests, hosted with pleasure by people who opened over the last years along the open borders. They show what they possess, proud to have no secrets and speak enthusiastically and with deep respect about their wine. They do it as philosophers do when they try to explore the nature of being. Profit isn't their immediate objective, they look for the way towards it. Decorations are left aside to reach the core, the centre of knowledge that already the ancient Romans enclosed into the saying "in vino veritas" (in the wine there lies the truth). The Tements and Polz, the Sattlers and Sabbatis belong to the new generation of winegrowers, who have rediscovered the earthiness without having the brown and lumpy soil stuck on their feet. That's the way they produce wine. They succeed in filling the landscape into the bottles and playfully fiddle about it to make connoisseurs wander along the wine trail in their memories, when they open a bottle of Morillon at home even months later. Everything the country offers is in that wine: body, strength, finesse, and above all an enormous lust. It's an erotic feeling that has absorbed so much and that flows over and gives birth to dreams. Delicate dreams, you have to approach carefully. They don't like a direct confrontation, being as brief as the smell of freshly roasted chestnuts, like the taste of ripening quinces. These dreams are soft like the dresses of light lavishly worn by the hills everyday. They are filled with touches and of being touched.

Just as you would visit a famous dome in its silence and look forward to hearing the sound of the organ, or as you would travel to Venice in November thinking of the colourful carnival masks, so you visit Southern Styria – apart from August – in the springtime. It is then that the young grass and the first stinging nettles make you feel the intensity of nature after a long and odourless winter. Such happy emotions make you forget the long way from the hard border to the easy lightness of the place.

Klapotetz im Abenddunst nahe Leutschach
Klapotetz in the evening mist near Leutschach, – the typical Styrian rattling wind wheel to scare off birds

Blick von der Fötschacher Höhenstraße auf die herbstliche Weinlandschaft
View from the Fötschach mountain street over the autumnal wine-growing area

Sonnige Winterabendstimmung in der Nähe von Ratsch
A winter sunset near Ratsch

Die südsteirische Weinstraße – wo die Weingärten in den Himmel wachsen
The Southern Styrian wine trail – where vineyards nearly touch the skies

Frühling in Steinbach
Springtime in Steinbach

Die größte Weintraube aus Glas, von Willi Trojan aus Langegg geschaffen, bei der Buschenschank Eory

The world's greatest grape made of glass, created by Willi Trojan of Langegg, near Eory's Buschenschank (wine tavern)

Abendstimmung über der südsteirischen Weinstraße
After sunset on the Southern Styrian wine trail

Kapelle im südoststeirischen Weinland nahe Bad Gleichenberg
Chapel on the wine trail near Bad Gleichenberg

Weinlandschaft Kapfenstein an der Weinstraße
The wine-growing area of Kapfenstein on the wine trail

Abendliche Weinlandschaft: Blick von Sernau in Richtung Karnerberg
Vineyards at dusk: View from Sernau towards Karnerberg

Ein Wintermärchen

A winter fairy tale

Herbst im Weinland
Autumn in the wine-growing region

Schilchertraube im Weingut Deutsch-Maier, Bad Gams
A bunch of Schilcher grapes in the wine-growing estate of Deutsch-Maier, Bad Gams

„Holder-Einsatz“ im Weingut Lackner-Tinnacher, Steinbach
A ”holder“ at work in the vineyard of Lackner-Tinnacher, Steinbach

Karin Reiterer bei der Schilchertraubenlese in der Nähe von Wies
Karin Reiterer collecting the Schilcher grapes near Wies

Spätherbst im Bad Gamser Schilcherland
Late autumn in the famous "Schilcher country" of Bad Gams

Buttenträger Christian Kugl im Gebiet Grasnitzberg bei Spielfeld
Christian Kugl carrying his container full with grapes in the area of Grasnitzberg near Spielfeld

Kleine Lesehilfe im Schilcherland
Mother's little helper at the grape harvest in the "Schilcher country"

Weinlese im Sausal
bei Mitteregg

Grape harvest in the valley of
Sausal near Mitteregg

... aber die Trauben hängen zu hoch
... but it's just sour grapes

Fritz Tinnacher kontrolliert den Reifegrad seiner Trauben
Fritz Tinnacher supervising the ripeness of his grapes

Idyll an der Sausaler Weinstraße
Idyllic scene on the Sausal wine trail

Der Moment zwischen Lese und Pressen

The moment between harvest and pressing of the grapes

Alte Tradition in moderner Zeit – Monika Elsnegg mit Butte und Handy
Old tradition in modern time – Monika Elsnegg with her grape container and mobile phone

Sanfter Pressvorgang nach alter Methode
Gentle way of traditional pressing

Johann Jöbstl an seiner Baumpresse nahe Sernau
Johann Jöbstl at his wooden wine-pressing machine

Johann Tieber aus Grubtal, einer der letzten Faßbinder in der Region
Johann Tieber from Grubtal, one of the last producers of barrels in the whole region

Im Weinkeller von Schloss Seggau
In the wine-cellar of Seggau castle

Mußestunde im Weingarten
Leisure hour in the vineyard

Waschtag am Demmerkogel bei Kitzeck
Washday on the Demmerkogel near Kitzeck

Grafische Weingartenlandschaften an der Sausaler Weinstraße
Graphic artwork in the vineyards on the Sausal wine trail

Weingarten am Zieregg
Vineyard on the Zieregg

Farbstimmungen im Spätherbst
Shades of colours in late autumn

Alles Schilcher in Bad Gams
Schilcher grapes all over the place in Bad Gams

Die Theresienkapelle am Demmerkogel
Theresia's Chapel on the Demmerkogel

Weinlandschaft nach der Lese in der Nähe von Langegg
Wine-growing area after the harvest near Langegg

Kitzeck aus der Luft
Aerial view of Kitzeck

Winter im Sulztal
Wintertime in the Sulztal

An der Weinstraße
In the very heart of the wine trail

Klassisches Motiv an der südsteirischen Weinstraße
Typical scenery on the wine trail of Southern Styria

Sonnenuntergang im hügeligen Weinland
Sunset in the wine-growing region of the Styrian hills

Regenstimmung über Kitzeck
A rainy day in Kitzeck

Geräteschuppen im Schilcherland
Toolshed in the “Schilcher country”

An der Klöcher Weinstraße
On the Klöch wine trail

Einer der stillen Plätze im Weinland
One of the silent spots in the wine-growing region

Geometrie der Weinzeilen in Steinbach
Geometry of a vineyard in Steinbach

„Sturmzeit“

At the time of the ”Sturm“ –
a popular intermediate product of
the alcoholic fermentation process

Manfred Tement bei der Faßprobe
Manfred Tement controlling his barrels

Gemütliche Stimmung bei der Buchenschank Pichler-Schober in Mitteregg
Relaxed atmosphere in the Buschenschank Pichler-Schober in Mitteregg

Eine kleine Stärkung
beim Musizieren

A little refreshment
after playing the concertina

Eine köstliche Brettljause gibt es hier überall ...

A delicious snack of homemade Styrian specialities you can get here everywhere ...

In einer Buchenschank bei Bad Gams

In a Buschenschank near Bad Gams

Beim Kieslinger am Kogelberg
At Kieslinger's at the Kogelberg

Weinlagerung auf steirisch

The Styrian way of keeping
a bottle of wine

Maroni-Zeit: Im Herbst werden überall Kastanien gebraten

At the time of the ”Maroni“: in autumn (sweet) chestnuts are roasted everywhere

Romatik pur im Jaglhof bei Sernau
A romantic dream at the Jaglhof near Sernau

Abendstimmung über Kitzeck
Atmospheric evening in Kitzeck

Ein südsteirisches Original
A real South Styrian character

Der Scherer-Kogel in der Nähe von Gamlitz

Scherer mountain near Gamlitz

Detail einer Weinkellertüre
Detail of a door to a wine cellar

Schmuckvolles Winzerhaus
Decorated house of a wine-grower

Südsteirisches Stillleben
Still life from Southern Styria

Altsteirisches Plumpsklo
Traditional Styrian loo

Der größte Klapotetz der Welt am Demmerkogel
The world's biggest Klapotetz on the Demmerkogel

Herbststimmung an der Klöcher Weinstraße
The first touch of autumn on the Klöch wine trail

Blick auf das Hügelland an der slowenischen Grenze
View over the hilly countryside near the Slovenian border

Im steirischen Himmelreich beim Weingut Christian Reiterer in Lamberg
In the Styrian "Kingdom of Heaven" on Christian Reiterer's wine-growing estate

Alte Jahrgänge im Weinkeller von Seggau
Old vintages in the wine-cellar of Seggau

Im Flaschenkeller des Georgi-Schlössls in Ehrenhausen
View of the wine-cellar of the Georgi-Schlössl in Ehrenhausen

Karl Thaler beim Verkosten seines neuen Shiraz, Maierhofberg
Karl Thaler tasting his new Shiraz, Maierhofberg

Kathi Tscheppe testet den neuen Welschriesling
Kathi Tscheppe controlling the new Welschriesling

Herbert Hirtners Weinkostkeller in Sernau
Herbert Hirtner's wine tasting cellar in Sernau

Gesamtsteirische Vinothek in St. Anna am Aigen
St. Anna am Aigen: A vinotheque offering wines from all Styrian regions

SALO
ÖSTERREICHS
Koller
79

Kellermalereien bei Johann Jöbstl in Sernau
Cellar paintings at Johann Jöbstl's in Sernau

Im Schilcherweinkeller von Johann Koller, Wildbach
In the Schilcher wine vaults of Johann Koller, Wildbach

Faßkeller der Familie Winkler-Hermaden in Kapfenstein
Barrel vaults of Winkler-Hermaden in Kapfenstein

Steirischer Wein – der Sonne am nächsten
Styrian wine – as close to the sun as you con get

Die steilsten Weinhänge sind
zweifellos in der Südsteiermark

The steepest vineyards can
undoubtedly be found here in the
southern part of Styria

Frühling im Grenzland

Springtime in border country

Österreich

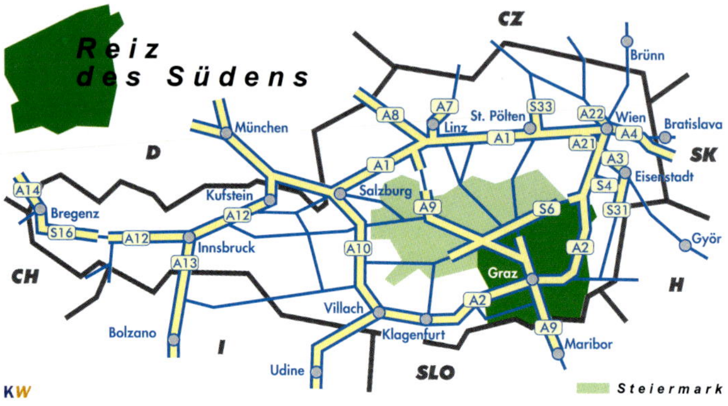

Mountainbike/Trekking

- Murradweg
- Radl-Trekking Tour
- Mur-Drau Radweg
- Grenz-Panoramaweg
- Wandergebiet
- Wanderdorf

Weinstraßen

- Schilcher Weinstraße
- Südsteirische Weinstraße
- Sausaler Weinstraße
- Südoststeirische Hügelland-weinstraße
- Klöcher Weinstraße
- Thermenland Weinstraße
- Oststeirische Römerweinstraße
- Klapotetzstraße

Themen-Erlebnispunkte

- Thermen
- Golf
- Kürbis
- Vinotheken
- Schlösser
- Museen
- Schiffmühle
- Reiten
- Ballonfahren
- Paragleiten

Erlebnisstraßen

- Almenstraße
- Apfelstraße
- Blumenstraße

Topographie

- A9 Autobahn mit Anschlußstelle
- Bundesstraße
- Verbindungsstraße
- Eisenbahn
- Gewässer
- Seilbahnen
- Ortsgrundriß
- **LEIBNITZ** Städte
- **Paldau** Märkte
- ***Rettenegg*** Dörfer